From
Rabble to Riches

By WaliWaza P.E.™

WaliWaza LLC · California

Published by
WaliWaza LLC
Los Altos, CA 94024

Library of Congress Control Number: 2010916095
ISBN 978-0-9830826-0-6

Manufactured in the United States.
CPSIA Compliance Information: Batch # 1110
For further information contact RJ Communications, NY, NY, 800-621-2556.

www.waliwaza.com

To the children who inspired me to write this; to Rotary International for its inspiration in global public service; and to our founding fathers, parents, family, teachers, and all people who think about and commit their lives to helping us achieve our full potential.

Life for the Rabble was hard as can be;
no games, no books, no color TV.

The Rabble worked hard each and every day,
cutting the wheat and baling the hay.

At night they would sleep in homes made of mud:
but when the rains came, those mud homes would flood.

The Rabble were generally hungry and wet.
With no time for fun, they were very upset.

Wali was Rabble - like the others - that's true;
but he was special and different - unique through and through.

Wali planned for the future and dreamt of a day
when the Rabble were happy and had time to play.

Anxious to learn, he would stop you to ask,
"How does it work?" or "Why do that task?"

He used what he learned to draw many strange things,
like robotic dogs and machines with big wings.

Wali wanted some help to make his big dreams come true,
  but those willing to help were indeed very few.

The Rabble simply did not understand,
  so no one was willing to give Wali a hand.

Wali was different, and so the Rabble made fun:
  they laughed at the dreams of this inventive one.

When Wali went out
to ask him for aid,

even the mayor his
feelings betrayed.

"Stop all this
dreaming. Stop
wasting my time.

Just go do your
chores, and
all will be fine."

But Wali could not let go of his vision.
 Alone he would work - he'd made his decision.

To the forest he went to build his machine:
 an invention the Rabble had never foreseen.

But there was something else, odd and quite strange...

...Wali himself was starting to change!

The Mayor proclaimed: "Wali, I must speak!"

"If you don't start your chores, your year will be bleak."

"If you don't prep for the harvest and your house falls apart,
you'll be starving and cold and stuck out in the dark.

I am warning you now - so LET ME BE CLEAR;
I won't come to your aid and I won't shed a tear."

But in spite of their doubt, Wali trusted his dream,
and when spring came around he rolled out his machine .

He planted four times what he'd planted years past,
and when harvest time came he worked eight times as fast.

His stomach was full for once in his life,
and he had time to play with his kids and his wife.

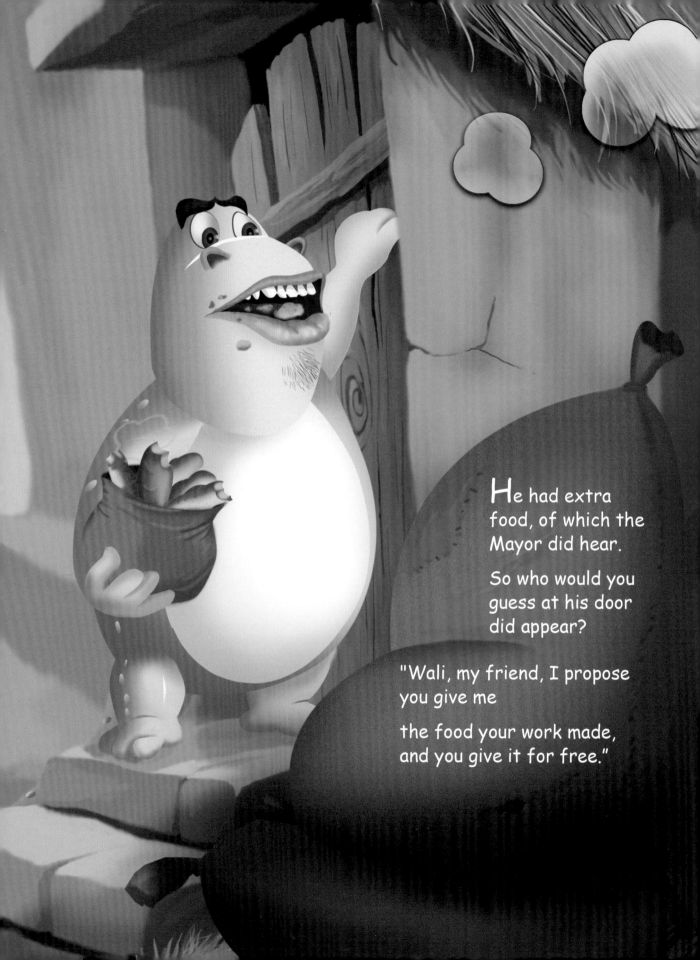

He had extra food, of which the Mayor did hear.

So who would you guess at his door did appear?

"Wali, my friend, I propose you give me

the food your work made, and you give it for free."

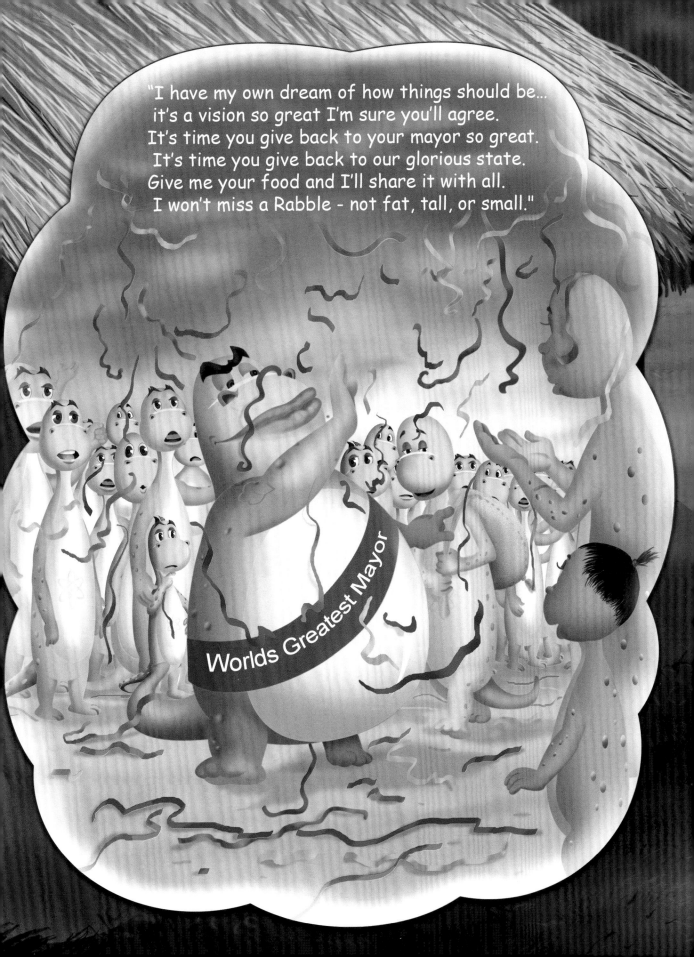

But Wali considered the numbers in "all"
and noticed the portions would be very small.

Each Rabble would get but barely a crumb.
Hungry they'd stay, upset and quite glum.

ali, a thinker, wanted more
r the town,

he put forth a challenge at
nich the mayor did frown.

ali proclaimed: "For a year
will feed

ny Rabble that tries to do a
reat deed."

THE GREAT CHALLENGE

Now good Mrs. Carpenter, how she loved to build.
She had a great gift; she was really quite skilled.

But she never had time to work with her woo[d]
and she felt out of place and misundersto[od.]

She hated to farm,
so she threw down her spade
and she went to Wali
to offer a trade...

For food for a year she would build him a house,
with warm and dry rooms for his kids and his spouse.

Once news of Mrs. Carpenter began to spread,
the Rabble their shyness started to shed.

Among all the Rabble, no other could beat
good Mr. Farmer's production of wheat.

But the mayor had taken the extra away,
and no one is sure where it went to this day.

So Wali and Farmer planned a fair trade:

Farmer would get the machine as an aide,

and Wali would get half the food that was made.

Mrs. Carpenter's skills were quickly expanding.
The house that she built was truly outstanding.

And with Wali's machine, Farmer's skill was set free.
That year he grew food to feed twenty three!

Wali was pleased and his challenge repeated,

which this time the Rabble excitedly greeted.

As the Rabble their differences began to explore,
they began on their own to trade and do more.

Miller built a machine to process the wheat,
and Miner mined coal to provide the town heat.

Smith built his tools day in and day out,
while Mason built walls of brick very stout.

One at a time the Rabble started to change,
and soon being different no longer seemed strange.

Even the mayor, who once was so huffy,

learned to make cakes moist and quite fluffy.

He used his great skill to bake for the town,

and discovered that cooking got rid of his frown.

Now that the Rabble love what they do,
you may see a change in more than a few.

The Rabble discovered being different is dandy,
and that using your skills can make you quite handy.

The happiest of all have found their own niche,
and found helping others can make you quite rich.

Trading their skills helped them all get ahead.
No longer Rabble - they're now warm and well fed.

How can you make the world better for all?
It's good to think big, but it's O.K. to start small.

Think of your family and the people you know.
Can you help them today? How 'bout tomorrow?